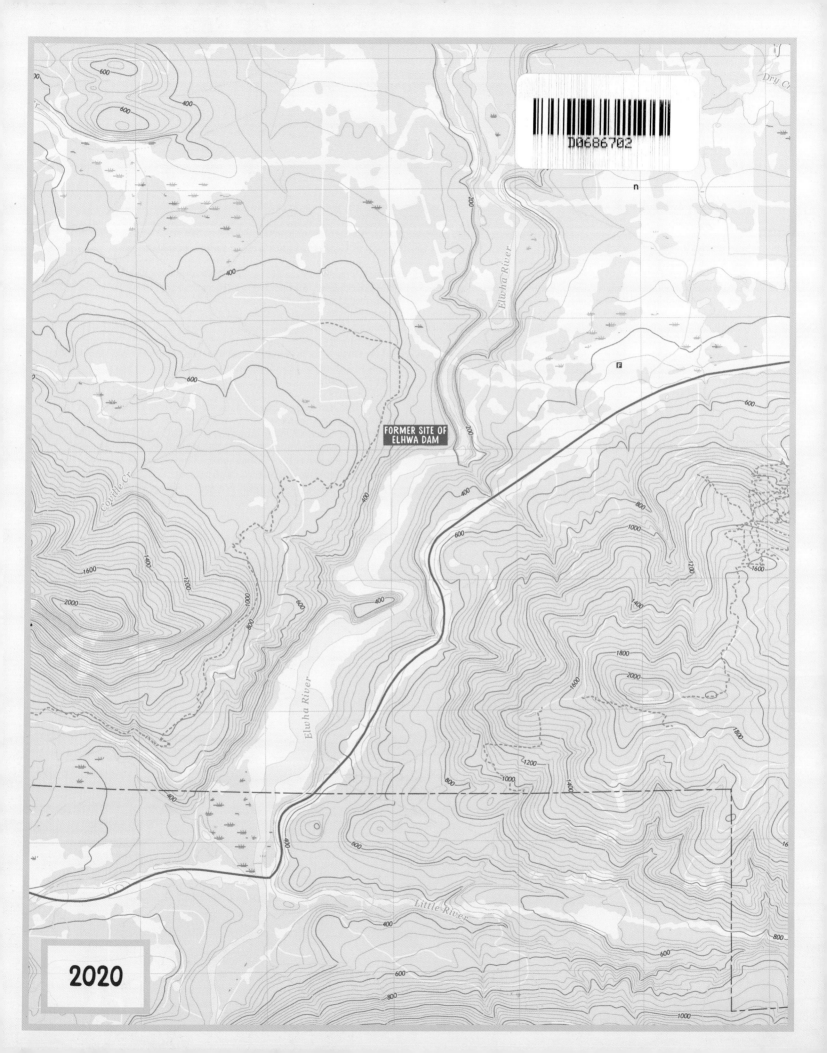

For Theo Claire, who found initial inspiration as a
voice for our planet in a children's book —P.N.

Millbrook Press™
An imprint of Lerner Publishing Group, Inc.
241 First Avenue North
Minneapolis, MN 55401 USA

For reading levels and more information, look up this title at
www.lernerbooks.com.

Additional images by: *Lady of the Mountain Breaks the Dam*, by Roger
Fernandes, courtesy of the Lower Elwha Klallam Tribe, p. 45; North
Olympic Heritage, Bert Kellogg Photograph Collection, p. 46 (both); Joel
Rogers/Getty Images, p. 47 (top right); Kate Benkert/USFWS, p. 47 (top
left); Olympic National Park, p. 47 (center); Russell Illig/Getty Images,
p. 47 (bottom); endpaper maps courtesy of USGS.

Designed by Danielle Carnito.
Main body text set in Buccardi Std.
Typeface provided by Monotype Typography.
The illustrations in the book were created with pencil, ink, and Procreate.

Library of Congress Cataloging-in-Publication Data

Names: Newman, Patricia, 1958– author. | Donovan, Natasha, illustrator.
Title: A river's gifts : the mighty Elwha River reborn / Patricia Newman ;
   illustrated by Natasha Donovan.
Description: Minneapolis : Millbrook Press, [2023] | Includes
   bibliographical references. | Audience: Ages 8-12 | Audience: Grades
   4-6 | Summary: "There's more to a river than meets the eye. The story
   of the Elwha River in Washington State is one of both environmental
   harm and restoration involving advocacy, persistence, cooperation, and
   hope" —Provided by publisher.
Identifiers: LCCN 2021056741 (print) | LCCN 2021056742 (ebook) |
   ISBN 9781541598706 (library binding) | ISBN 9781728462615 (ebook)
Subjects: LCSH: Restoration ecology—Washington (State)—Elwha River—
   Juvenile literature. | Wildlife management—Washington (State)—Elwha
   River—Juvenile literature. | Wildlife habitat improvement—Washington
   (State)—Elwha River—Juvenile literature. | Natural history—Washington
   (State)—Elwha River—Juvenile literature.
Classification: LCC QH105.W2 N49 2023 (print) | LCC QH105.W2
   (ebook) | DDC 639.909797/99—dc23/eng/20211122

LC record available at https://lccn.loc.gov/2021056741
LC ebook record available at https://lccn.loc.gov/2021056742

Manufactured in the United States of America
1-48056-48737-2/4/2022

A RIVER'S GIFTS

THE MIGHTY ELWHA RIVER REBORN

PATRICIA NEWMAN

ILLUSTRATED BY

NATASHA DONOVAN

MILLBROOK PRESS
Minneapolis

Mountain snow melts. *Plip . . . plop . . . plip.*
The drops flow together as trickling streams,
and then unite as one river.

For thousands of years the roar and thunder of this river
tumbled through steep canyons,
carrying rocks, branches, gravel
and winding a twisting path through the forest.
Always, it flowed north to the sea
sharing its gifts with
animals, plants, and people
who cared for it in return.

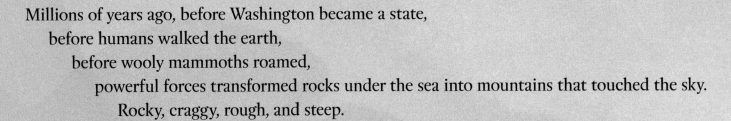

Millions of years ago, before Washington became a state,
before humans walked the earth,
before wooly mammoths roamed,
powerful forces transformed rocks under the sea into mountains that touched the sky.
Rocky, craggy, rough, and steep.

Ice fields blanketed mountains and lowlands,
and fed smaller glaciers that marched slowly forward,
carving the narrow canyons
and broad valleys
where the Elwha River would soon flow.

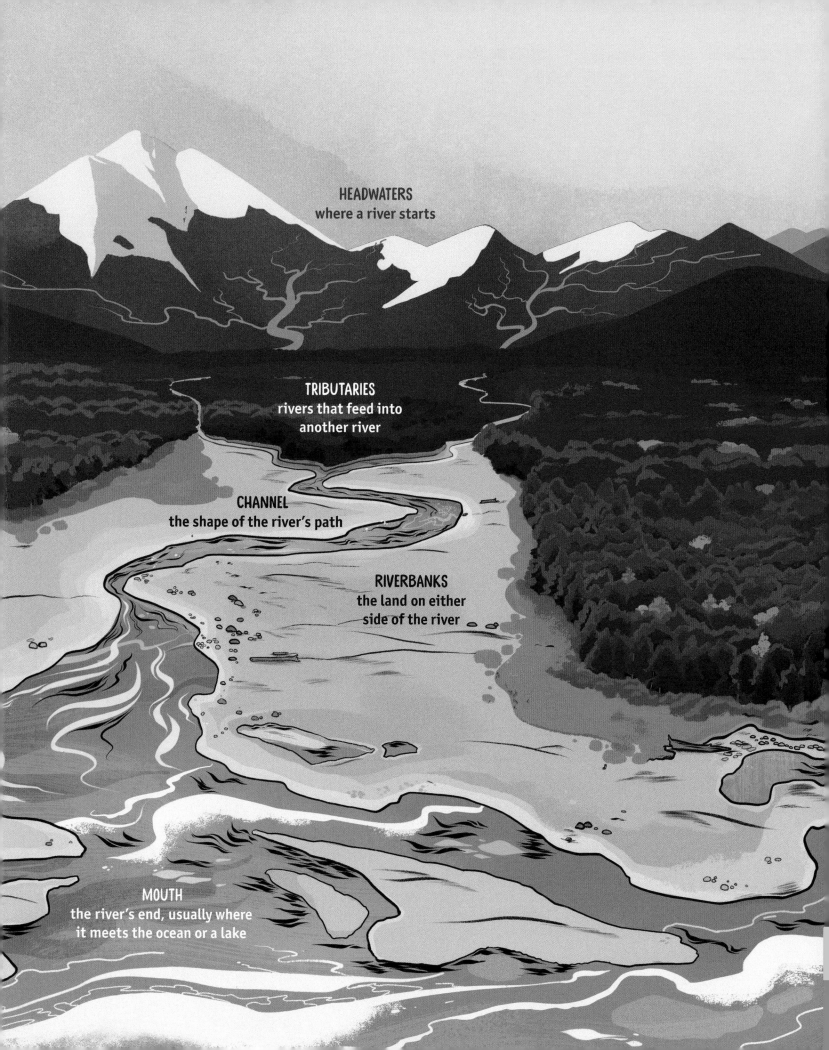

HEADWATERS
where a river starts

TRIBUTARIES
rivers that feed into
another river

CHANNEL
the shape of the river's path

RIVERBANKS
the land on either
side of the river

MOUTH
the river's end, usually where
it meets the ocean or a lake

Year after year, the mighty Elwha churned with salmon
thrashing against the current,
leaping up waterfalls.
The rushing river called them home from the sea.
Bears, otters, and eagles caught some of them.
The rest laid eggs in shallow riffles before dying.
Their bodies enriched the soil that grew the forest
that fed the mice, the deer, and the elk.
In spring, millions of salmon eggs hatched.
The young fish preyed on tiny insects in the river,
and grew and grew, until the time came to swim for the sea.
On their journey, some became meals for other fish and birds.
The river fed the salmon, and the salmon fed the river.

A SAFE PLACE FOR YOUNG SALMON

Alevins (newborns) usually hatch in spring and live close to their redd (underwater gravel nest) for a few months.

Males and females die soon after spawning.

Alevins become fry (juveniles) and stay in the river for up to a year.

Males compete to fertilize eggs. The female covers the eggs with small rocks.

Adult females swim upstream to find good redd sites. They turn on their sides to dig with their tails.

When fry swim for the sea, they become silvery smolts with scales. They feed at the mouth of the river and adjust to saltwater life.

Salmon spend up to seven years in the ocean. They follow scents, chemical clues, and even the sun to return to their home river to spawn (lay and fertilize eggs).

When the Lower Elwha Klallam Tribe arrived, the salmon fed them too.
They call themselves the Strong People,
and the river flows in their blood.
The Strong People caught salmon in traps along the river,
grateful for the abundance,
taking only what they needed,
and allowing others to escape upstream to spawn.

The river also nurtured life on its banks.

    Plants for the Strong People's medicines;

        deer and elk for their meat, clothing, and tools;

            spicy-smelling cedars for woven baskets and sturdy canoes;

               and sweet berries to savor.

For thousands of years, river, forest, salmon, and Strong People nourished one another.

    Until 1790, when the current changed.

THE CONTEST

One day many tribes held a contest to see who could lift a big log to the top of an unfinished longhouse. Each tribe chose their strongest men, but none could lift the log.

The mighty Klallams remembered that logs float in water. They rolled the big log into the river and the strongest men waded in after it. They floated the log onto their shoulders and walked out of the river.

The other tribes praised the mighty Klallams' strength and wisdom. They all shouted, "Nəxʷsƛ̓áy̓əm! Nəxʷsƛ̓áy̓əm!" which means, "Strong People! Strong People!"

Strangers arrived on horseback. More arrived by wagon.

These were not Strong People.

They did not understand the river's gifts.

The strangers saw wilderness to tame.

They replaced tangled berry bushes with rows of crops.

They felled trees sheltering birds and insects to build homes of their own.

Their axes carved out a ragged frontier town
of muddy streets dotted with tree stumps and lowing cattle.

The strangers wrote new laws.
    Strong People cannot own land.
    Strong People cannot fish.
Laws that separated the Strong People from their food,
    their homes, their culture.
Laws that made them outsiders in their own land.

And then in 1890, Thomas Aldwell came to town,
    with big plans for the river's natural abundance
        and inexhaustible energy.

He built a dam on the Elwha River.
    A marvel of engineering to harness the thundering water
        and make something new called electricity.

            Electric lights in people's homes!
            Electric tram cars in town!
            Electric-powered sawmills for new jobs!

BUILDING BY HAND

When construction on the Elwha Dam began in 1910, today's modern power equipment didn't exist. The workers dug, hammered, sawed, and fastened everything by hand.

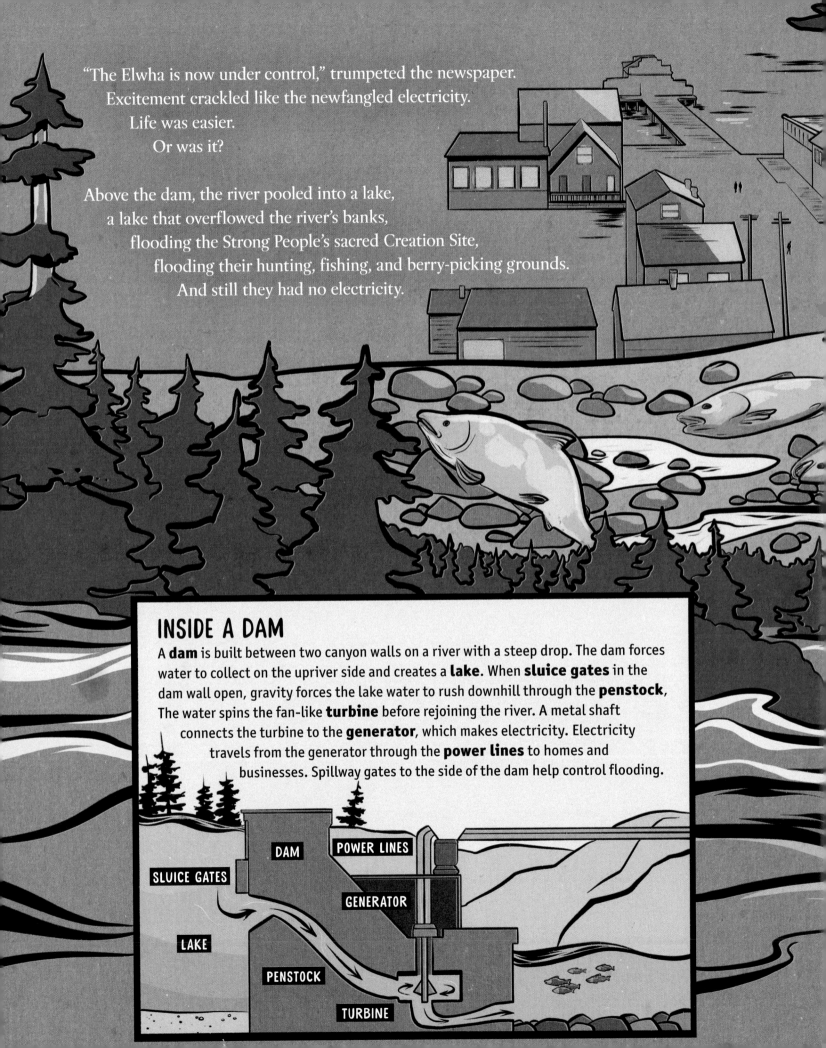

"The Elwha is now under control," trumpeted the newspaper.
Excitement crackled like the newfangled electricity.
Life was easier.
Or was it?

Above the dam, the river pooled into a lake,
a lake that overflowed the river's banks,
flooding the Strong People's sacred Creation Site,
flooding their hunting, fishing, and berry-picking grounds.
And still they had no electricity.

INSIDE A DAM

A **dam** is built between two canyon walls on a river with a steep drop. The dam forces water to collect on the upriver side and creates a **lake**. When **sluice gates** in the dam wall open, gravity forces the lake water to rush downhill through the **penstock**, The water spins the fan-like **turbine** before rejoining the river. A metal shaft connects the turbine to the **generator**, which makes electricity. Electricity travels from the generator through the **power lines** to homes and businesses. Spillway gates to the side of the dam help control flooding.

POWER LINES

DAM

SLUICE GATES

GENERATOR

LAKE

PENSTOCK

TURBINE

Below the dam, the river straightened.
Shallow riffles and rocks disappeared.
Warm lake water spilled into the river.
Salmon could not survive.

River, forest, salmon, and Strong People could no longer nourish each other.

Wild salmon that had traveled to sea before the dam was built returned to spawn.
   Fish must be allowed to pass! state law said.
      Salmon jumped at the base of the immovable dam to reach their spawning sites,
         day after day
            until they finally died.

State workers who were supposed to protect the fish did not protest.

Instead, they asked Thomas Aldwell to build a hatchery
   to farm the salmon caught at the base of the dam.
      Fish eggs were gathered and fertilized for a few years,
         but the hatchery soon failed
            because not enough salmon returned from the sea.

Only the Strong People and a handful of townspeople objected.

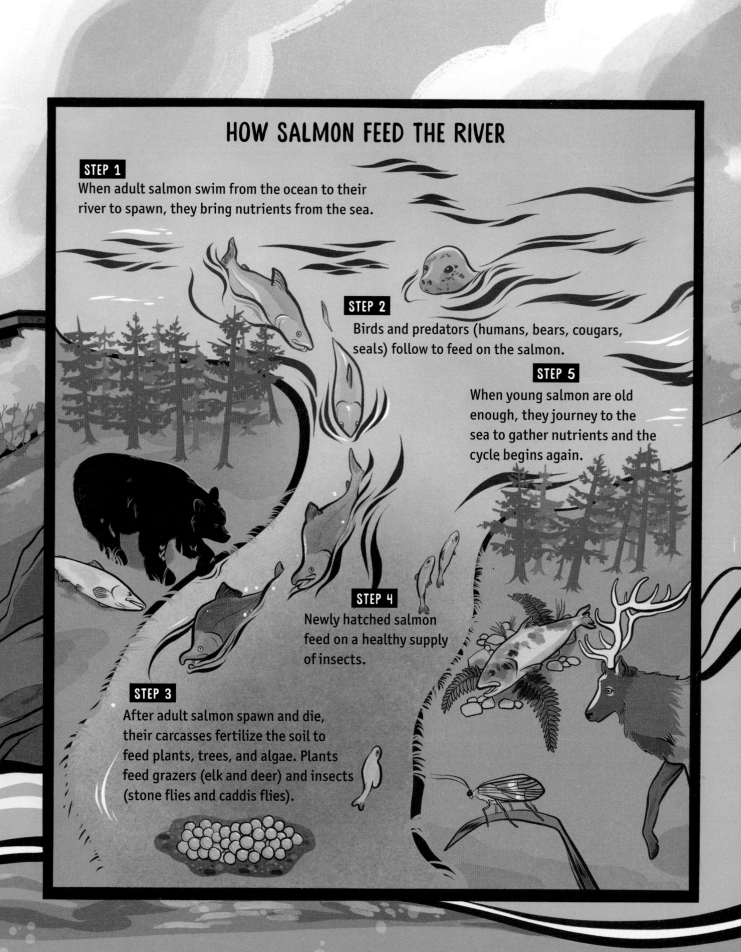

HOW SALMON FEED THE RIVER

STEP 1
When adult salmon swim from the ocean to their river to spawn, they bring nutrients from the sea.

STEP 2
Birds and predators (humans, bears, cougars, seals) follow to feed on the salmon.

STEP 5
When young salmon are old enough, they journey to the sea to gather nutrients and the cycle begins again.

STEP 4
Newly hatched salmon feed on a healthy supply of insects.

STEP 3
After adult salmon spawn and die, their carcasses fertilize the soil to feed plants, trees, and algae. Plants feed grazers (elk and deer) and insects (stone flies and caddis flies).

While salmon struggled, the town thrived.
New homes.
New businesses.
New jobs.

More electricity! cried the owners of a new paper mill.

A new dam was built in Glines Canyon,
    upriver from the first dam,
        with another lake that flooded land long protected by the Strong People.
            Another dam that prevented fish from passing.

The grind and clang of the dams' power plants silenced the roar and thunder of the river.

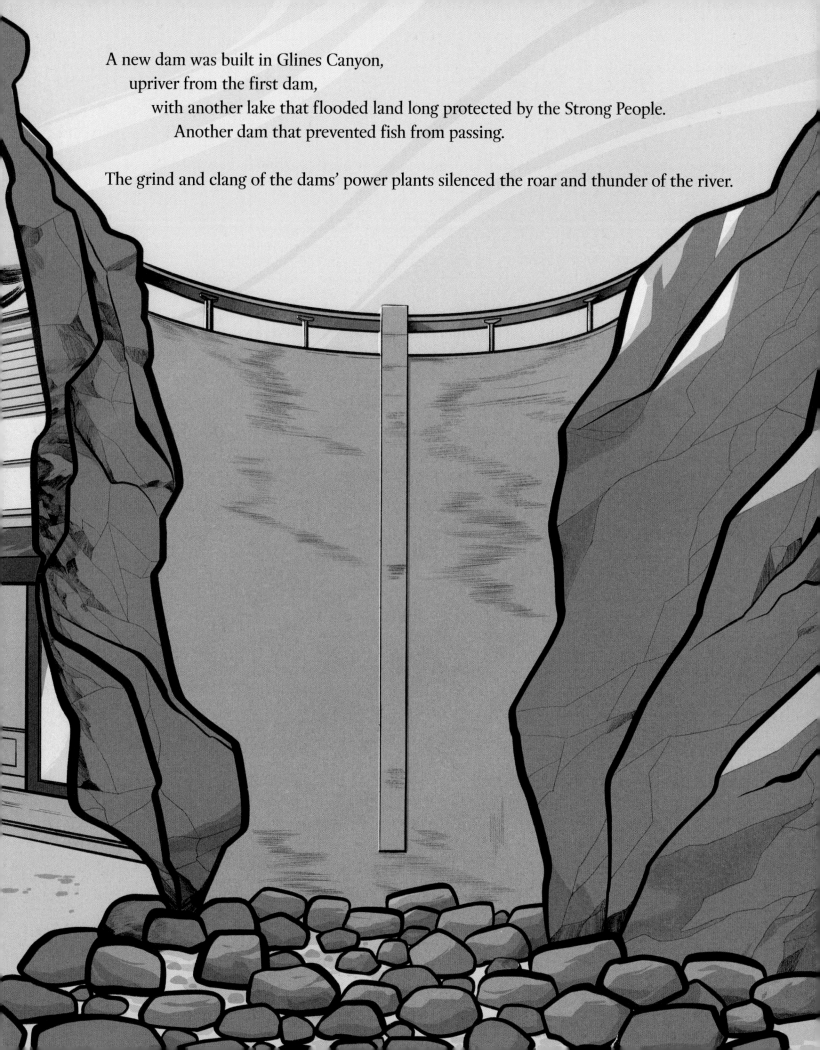

The dams halted the usual tumble of rocks,
　　branches,
　　　　stones,
　　　　　　and gravel
that protected the river's banks and provided habitats for its wildlife and plants.

Riverbanks eroded, taking trees and bushes with them,
　　small stones that protected salmon eggs vanished,
　　　　and clam beds at the river's mouth washed away on the tides.
Without salmon, eagles left the trees,
　　bears moved to higher ground, and
　　　　river otters, raccoons, and woodpeckers searched elsewhere for food.
And when the gates of the dams opened to make electricity,
　　they released too much
　　　　or too little water,
　　　　　　which flooded or starved the river's wildlife and its people.

OLYMPIC NATIONAL PARK

In Olympic National Park, hikers and birders scale magnificent mountain peaks. They travel winding paths in the old growth temperate rain forest dripping with mist. Boaters paddle the park's lowland lakes, fishermen stand on the banks of its rushing rivers, and beachcombers scour its tidelands.

Protected as a National Forest Reserve since 1897, President Franklin D. Roosevelt later declared it a national park in 1938. When the park's boundaries expanded to include Glines Canyon Dam in 1940, more than 85 percent of the Elwha River's watershed fell under the park's protection. Without Olympic National Park, there probably would have been no Elwha River Restoration Project.

As the town grew, larger and more modern dams on other
rivers sent electricity to its people and businesses.
By the 1940s, the Elwha's dams were old-fashioned,
outdated,
unimportant.

Still, they blocked the river.

Meanwhile, the Strong People continued to fight for the right to fish,
    for their culture,
        for their way of life.

In 1974, they won. But few salmon returned from the sea.
The Strong People opened their own hatchery,
    hoping the fish could thrive
        between the Elwha Dam and the mouth of the river.

And then the unexpected happened.
The license for Glines Canyon Dam needed renewing like an overdue library book.
    But Olympic National Park had grown, and the dam now stood within its borders.
    Renewing the license might not be possible!

        The Strong People saw their chance to save their river.
        Environmental groups and other townspeople joined them.
    For sixteen years, they educated the US Congress about the Elwha River.
        How its salmon suffered.
        How the habitat suffered.
            How the people suffered without a free-flowing river.
                BOTH dams must go! they said.

In 1992, Congress agreed.
Victory! The Elwha River would once again flow free
   from headwaters to mouth.

OTHER DAMS REMOVED

More than 1,797 dams have been removed in the
US between 1912 and 2020 to restore free-flowing
rivers and revitalize their ecosystems. Many of
these dams, like the Elwha River dams, were old,
unsafe, and no longer served their communities.

But not everyone was happy.
Many people played in the lakes above the dams.
Their drinking water came from the lakes.
They worked at the paper mill.
Without the dams, where would they swim and kayak?
Would their drinking water be filled with river sediment?
What about their paper mill jobs?
Who would pay for dam removal?
They didn't want change!

For twelve more years, the Strong People,
politicians, fishermen, townspeople, and government leaders
gathered facts, wrote, debated, argued, and marched,
while salmon banged their snouts against the Elwha Dam.

Finally, the two sides agreed.
Build a factory to clean drinking water!
Save the jobs!
Remove both dams!

And the National Park Service agreed to pay for it all.

Removing the dams would be complicated.
   Experts from the park, the tribe, and their partners worked together.
   They wanted to compare the river with dams to the river without dams.

Water scientists inserted microchips in rocks to track the river's speed.
   They figured out how to release a thundering cascade of water and sediment
   that had been blocked by the dams for the last hundred years.

Fish scientists snorkeled in shallow water to count salmon
and followed fish with tracking devices.
They measured the water's temperature,
the depth of spawning pools,
and the amount of shade and sunlight on the water.

Wildlife scientists clipped birds' claws to test for ocean-based nutrients
and tracked bears and river otters
to find out how animals used the river habitat.

Dam removal day dawned cool and cloudy.
    For generations, the Strong People had prayed for the return of the river.
        Now their children would see the Elwha River
            the way their great-great-grandparents saw it.

In June 2011, the grind and clang of the two dams was forever silenced.
    Engineers began to drain the lakes above the dams.
        As the water level slowly dropped,
            one-hundred-year-old stumps emerged,
                from trees cut down to build the dams.
                    Their sap still smelled sharp and sweet.

The lake bottoms looked like moonscapes of fine silt.
But plant scientists were ready to transform them into lush riverbanks.
They had gathered seeds from native plants and sprouted them in greenhouses.

Tribal scientists, park scientists, and volunteers planted four hundred thousand plants
on eight hundred acres of lake bed
over seven years.

They had some help from birds
that carried forest seeds in their beaks or feathers
and deposited them at their next feeding spot.

SALMONBERRY

SALAL

RATTLESNAKE PLANTAIN

While planters planted and scientists gathered information, engineers removed the dams, piece by piece.

For nearly three years, the rat-a-tat of jackhammers and the boom of dynamite echoed through the canyons.

Sometimes the rat-a-tat boom fell quiet to keep the fish from suffocating under the tons of sediment flowing downstream.

REMOVING THE DAMS

Beginning in September 2011, construction workers lowered the two lakes to the bottoms of the spill gates. At Glines Canyon Dam, a huge jackhammer on a barge notched out sections of the dam little by little to drain the lake and remove the dam.

At the Elwha Dam, workers demolished each side of the dam separately. They built a temporary dam to hold back the river while they destroyed the left side of the dam. On the right side, they blasted the concrete spillway to make a temporary path for the river. Finally, they reshaped the channel to restore the river's natural path.

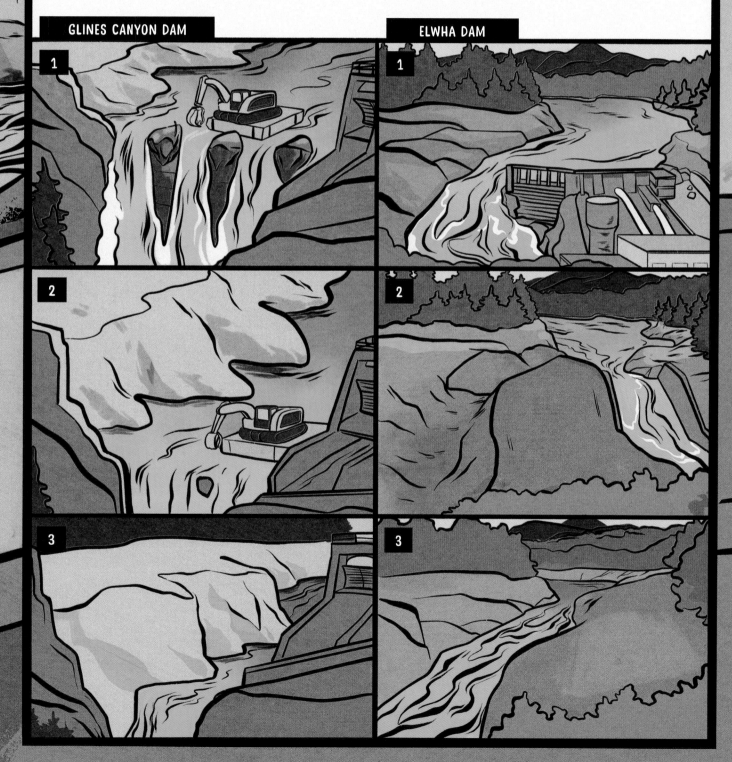

GLINES CANYON DAM

ELWHA DAM

Until finally the Elwha River once again flowed
wild,
free,
and almost completely protected within Olympic National Park.
The roar and thunder returned, ready to share its gifts.
Logs, branches, rocks, and sparkling bits of glacial sediment
created channels and pools perfect for spawning salmon.

For the first time in one hundred years, fish could travel from mouth to headwaters.
But would they return from the sea to spawn in the reborn Elwha River?

Everyone waited.

COYOTES

SHREWS

AMERICAN BLACK BEARS

RIVER
OTTERS

Three days later, one lone Chinook salmon cruised past the old damsites.
No one knew if more would follow.
Strong People stood on the banks of the Elwha
and performed their Salmon Ceremony to pray for a river churning with fish.

While they waited, they rediscovered their sacred Creation Site,
proud of the role they played in its return.

THE CREATION SITE

The Strong People believe life for their people began at a sacred rock on the banks of the Elwha River. Their Creator scooped them out of two holes in the rock shaped like coiled baskets. On this rock, the Creator bathed and blessed the people. In 2012, with the Elwha Dam only a memory, Strong People gathered at the sacred rock for the first time in a century. No one alive had ever before seen it.

More salmon returned than scientists expected,
    thrashing against the current,
        leaping up waterfalls.
            The rushing river calls them home to spawn.
When the eggs hatch, the young salmon prey on tiny insects,
    and grow and grow until the time comes to swim for the sea.
The old lake beds, now covered with shrubs and young trees, are alive
    with mice, beavers, elk, and raccoons.

Birds sing from the trees.
    River otters pad along the muddy riverbanks.
        Soon, bears will once again fish for salmon on the river's edge.

AMERICAN BLACK BEAR

KINGFISHER

MOUSE

PACIFIC SALMON (PINK, SOCKEYE, CHINOOK, COHO, CHUM)

Mountain snow melts. *Plip . . . plop . . . plip.*
The drops flow together as trickling streams
and then unite as one river.

Once more, the roar and thunder of the river
    tumbles through steep canyons,
        carrying rocks, branches, gravel,
            and winding a twisting path through the forest.
Always, it flows north to the sea
    sharing its gifts
        with animals, plants, and people
            who once again care for it in return.

FROM THE AUTHOR

Rivers have nourished our planet for eons. They flow through our history, our lives, and our livelihoods. They connect our cities and towns, provide drinking water, irrigate crops, slow flooding, and support wildlife.

We all live in a river basin—the area of land drained by a river and its tributaries. I live in the Sacramento River Basin in Sacramento, California, where the American and Sacramento Rivers meet. I love kayaking, hiking along the banks, or riding the rapids in a raft. Besides fun, Sacramento's rivers provide a habitat for salmon and other fish, and like the Elwha River, nourish our land-based habitats. Chances are you have a river, a stream, a creek, or a lake near you too. What is the name of your local river basin? How does it connect to your life?

The story of the Elwha River captured my attention because it demonstrates persistence, cooperation, drama, and the resilience of nature. It is a conservation story with a happy ending, but it's also a cautionary tale about the ripple effects humans have on wild places as we bend nature to our will.

When I visited the Elwha River to research this book, the dams were only a memory as the river burbled, rippled, and rushed from headwaters to sea. I hiked with a botanist to the replanted area that used to be Lake Aldwell. I spoke with a Lower Elwha Klallam tribal member and received private tours of the tribal fish hatchery and the tribal museum. I met with a photographer who documented the entire dam removal process with photos and film, and I interviewed a fish biologist at Olympic National Park. I also sifted through documents, photos, and computer files at local libraries and the Clallam County Historical Society.

I'm grateful to the many people who played a role in restoring the Elwha River. Their collaboration offers hope that if we rectify past environmental mismanagement, nature may respond, not only in the Pacific Northwest but throughout the world.

FROM THE ILLUSTRATOR

As an artist, every project brings me some new world to dive into, but it's a special privilege when I get to illustrate a book that feels like coming home.

I've lived on the West Coast my entire life, and I often find it quite hard to leave. My heart is here. I prefer to find my adventures just outside my door: in the silent mossy old-growth cathedrals overflowing with life, in the muck and squelch of a kelp-covered beach, in the delight of witnessing a dog salmon's final chaotic splashing leap toward her spawning grounds. With each excursion, I collect fascinating sensory experiences, and when I made the art for *A River's Gifts,* I got to draw on that catalog of wonders. The inspiration that I glean from this place is yet another one of its gifts.

As an illustrator, I believe that my first and most important job is to be a listener. In the process of making this book, many people—writers, editors, historians, environmentalists, scientists, community members—came together to tell a story of resilience, regrowth, and possibility. These storytellers are each unique and knowledgeable, and I thank them for giving me the opportunity to listen and to make art based on their invaluable work. A picture book is a tiny thing in this vast universe, but when you imagine all the communication and connection required . . . well, I think it's pretty exciting!

Immersing myself in this story has been a reminder that monumental change can happen, that ecosystems can be rebuilt, and that it is still very possible to foster reciprocal relationships with the land that feeds us, shelters us, and replenishes us.

A book can't come to life without its readers—so thank you most of all to the young people who pick up this book. Your curiosity is so important.

FROM SUZ BENNETT, TRIBAL MEMBER

For the Strong People, the Elwha River is more than rushing water, more even than home to the salmon that feed us. The Elwha is inspiration, the seed of our being. Here by the river, we were created. According to our traditional lore, the Lady of the Mountain lies in the Olympic Mountains, watching and waiting. If the world tips out of balance, she promises to rise from her mountain bed and return to help the Elwha people. In the depiction by Lower Elwha Klallam artist Roger Fernandes (*right*), the Lady of the Mountain breaks the dam after a hundred years of tribal endeavors and Thunderbird drives the salmon back up the river. We believe the tribal members who lobbied for dam removal and passed on before its completion have given the next seven generations physical, mental, and spiritual healing at the Elwha River.

TIMELINE

Thousands of years ago until the late 1800s: The Klallam are the largest tribe in the area. Their villages and camps dot the banks of the Elwha River.

1790: The first European explorers arrive, followed soon after by settlers.

1855: The Klallam are forced to sign over their land to the US government.

1890: Thomas Aldwell arrives in Port Angeles.

1909: President Theodore Roosevelt establishes the Olympic National Monument, the first step to becoming a national park.

1910: Construction begins on the Elwha Dam at mile 4.9 of the river. One year later, salmon disappear above the dam.

1914: The Elwha Dam begins generating electricity.

The Elwha Dam is nearly complete.

Building the Glines Canyon Dam.

1926: Construction begins on Glines Canyon Dam at mile 13.6 of the river.

1927: Glines Canyon Dam begins generating electricity.

1938: President Franklin D. Roosevelt establishes Olympic National Park.

1940: Olympic National Park's boundaries expand to include Glines Canyon Dam.

1979: The Glines Canyon Dam cannot be relicensed.

1986 to 1988: The Klallam tribe and environmentalists lobby for dam removal.

1992: President George H. W. Bush signs the Elwha River Ecosystem and Fisheries Restoration Act.

Demolishing the Elwha Dam.

Demolishing the Glines Canyon Dam.

1994: Opposition to dam removal grows.

2004: The dam removal project is given the final go-ahead.

2011: Power generation is shut down at the Elwha and Glines Canyon Dams. The lakes behind the dams are drained and demolition begins. Volunteers begin replanting the lake beds.

As Lake Mills drains, a volunteer plants a seedling.

2012: The Elwha Dam is gone. Glines Canyon Dam is half gone. Five months later, someone sees a Chinook salmon swimming above the former Elwha Dam's location.

2014: Glines Canyon Dam is gone, but a rockfall blocks the river.

2016: The rockfall is cleared away, and the river flows unobstructed.

The Elwha River once again flows wild and free.

FAVORITE SOURCES

Beirne, Matt, and Keith Lauderback, natural resources director/hatchery technician, interview by Patricia Newman, September 11, 2019.

Brown, Bruce. *Mountain in the Clouds: A Search for the Wild Salmon*. New York: Collier Books, 1982.

Claire, Theo, Elwha revegetation intern, interview by Patricia Newman, October 17, 2018.

Crain, Patrick, Acting Chief of Resource Management and Chief Fisheries Biologist, Olympic National Park, interview by Patricia Newman, September 11, 2019.

Crane, Jeff. *Finding the River: An Environmental History of the Elwha*. Corvallis: Oregon State University Press, 2011.

Gussman, John, photographer and filmmaker, interview by Patricia Newman, September 10, 2019.

Mapes, Lynda V. *Elwha: A River Reborn*. Seattle: Mountaineer Books, 2013.

Return of the River. DVD or stream. Directed by John Gussman and Jessica Plumb. 2014. For rental/stream: https://www.amazon.com/Return-River-Lower-Elwha-Klallam/dp/B01MUH4UGV.

Sager-Fradkin, Kim, Wildlife Program Manager, LEKT, interview by Patricia Newman, December 12, 2019.

Sampson, Jalen, Museum Host, Lower Elwha Klallam Museum at the Carnegie, interview by Patricia Newman, September 12, 2019.

Williams, Kim, Revegetation Supervisor and Climate Change Coordinator, interview by Patricia Newman, September 11, 2019.

MORE RIVER READS

Cherry, Lynne. *A River Ran Wild: An Environmental History*. New York: Houghton Mifflin Harcourt, 2002.

Cooper, Elisha. *River*. New York: Orchard Books, 2019.

Goes, Peter. *Rivers: A Visual History from River to Sea*. Wellington, NZ: Gecko, 2018.

Peters, Marilee. Illustrated by Kim Rosen. *10 Rivers That Shaped the World*. Toronto: Annick, 2015.

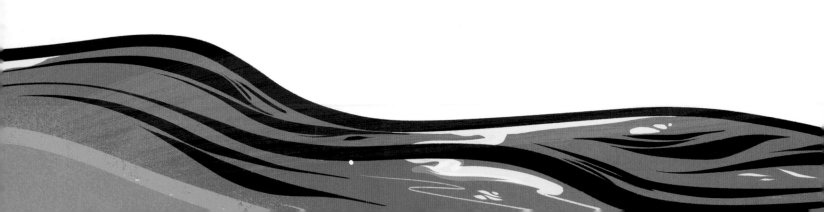

ACKNOWLEDGMENTS

Although the author and illustrator often receive the credit for a book, many people contribute to its development. This book would not have been possible without the following dedicated people:

- Theo Claire, whose summer internship on the Elwha sparked a conversation between Theo's mother, Allison Claire, and my husband, Kendall Newman. My wonderful husband recognized Theo's journey as the seed of a new book.

- The Lower Elwha Klallam Tribe and its Natural Resources Department who shared their passion and commitment for the Elwha River Restoration, including, Robert Elofson, Harvest Manager and Elwha River Restoration Director; Kim Williams, former Revegetation Supervisor and Climate Change Coordinator, who took me on a hike to the former Lake Aldwell; Kim Sager-Fradkin, Wildlife Program Manager; Suz Bennett, Enterprise Manager, Lower Elwha Klallam Tribe; Jalen Sampson, Museum Host, Elwha Klallam Museum at the Carnegie, who gave me a tour of the museum; Matt Beirne, Natural Resources Director; John Mahan, Fisheries Biologist and Hatchery Manager; and Keith Lauderback, hatchery technician who showed me how fish hatcheries work.

- Patrick Crain, Chief Fisheries Biologist, Olympic National Park, who shared his love of fish science and the Elwha as a career-making project.

- John Gussman, photographer and filmmaker, whose love of the area drove him to document in images and film every step of the restoration process.

- Bonnie Roos, Tribal Librarian for the Jamestown S'Klallam Tribe, who helped me research a particularly thorny historical issue.

- The marvelously organized women at the Clallam County Historical Society who scoured one hundred years of history for anything related to the Elwha River.

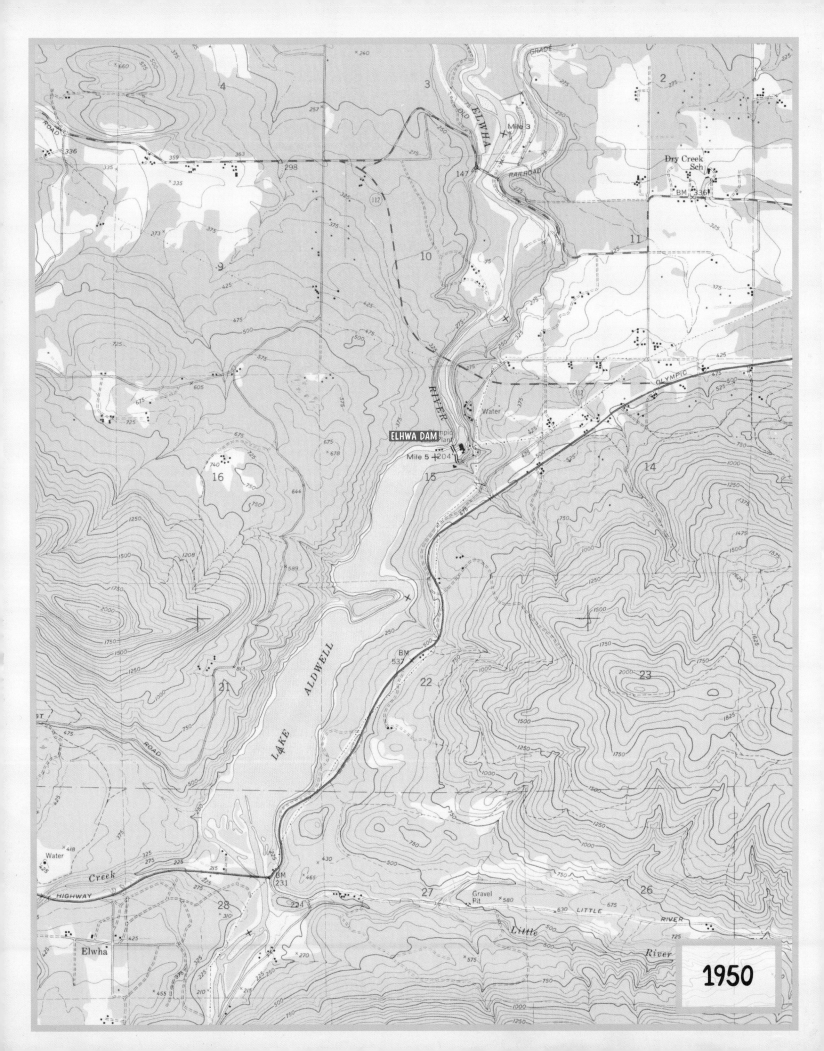